D1466116

MARC BROWN

ARTHUR'S UNDERWEAR

LITTLE, BROWN AND COMPANY
New York Boston

For all the kids
who insisted on an
underwear book

Little, Brown and Company
Hachette Book Group
1290 Avenue of the Americas, New York, NY 10104
Visit our website at www.lb-kids.com

Little, Brown and Company is a division of Hachette Book Group, Inc.
The Little, Brown name and logo are trademarks of Hachette Book Group, Inc.

The publisher is not responsible for websites (or their content) that are not owned by the publisher.

First Revised Edition: June 2011
First published in hardcover in September 1999 by Little, Brown and Company

Arthur® is a registered trademark of Marc Brown.

Library of Congress Cataloging-in-Publication Data

Brown, Marc Tolon.
Arthur's underwear/ Marc Brown.—1st ed.
p. cm.
Summary: It takes a really embarrassing moment in the school cafeteria
to cure Arthur of his fear of being caught in his underwear.
ISBN 978-0-316-11012-9 (hc) / ISBN 978-0-316-10619-1 (pb)
[1. Aardvark Fiction. 2. Embarrassment Fiction. 3. Schools Fiction.]
I. Title
PZ7.B81618Ary 1999
[E] — dc21   99-25702

20 19 18 17 16 15 14 13

APS

Printed in China

Binky Barnes was at the board doing a difficult problem. "That's correct," said Mr. Ratburn. "Very good."

Binky cheered, "Yes!" and dropped his chalk. As he bent down, the class heard a loud *RRRIPPP!*
Everyone laughed, except Mr. Ratburn. "Go to the office and ask Ms. Tingley to sew them up," he said.

That afternoon at softball practice, when Binky
came up to bat, Arthur thought about Binky in his
underwear and laughed.
During dinner, Mom asked, "Anything interesting
happen at school today?"
Arthur started to laugh.
"What's so funny?" asked D.W.
But Arthur couldn't stop laughing to answer.

The next morning, Arthur woke up late.
He hurried through breakfast and ran most of the way
to school.
"Sorry I'm late, Mr. Ratburn! I guess my alarm —"
Everyone burst out laughing.
"Mr. Read, being late is one thing," said Mr. Ratburn,
"but not wearing any trousers — *that* is quite another!"
Arthur looked down — and screamed!

Arthur's scream woke him up.
Wow, he thought, *what a horrible dream!*

In school, the class watched a science film. "The amoeba is a single-celled life form. . . ."
Arthur's eyelids began to droop.

Suddenly, an amoeba that looked a lot like Arthur appeared on the screen. Its pants fell down, showing its underwear.

"Help!" cried Arthur-Amoeba. "I need my pants!"
All the other amoebas started to laugh.

Arthur-Amoeba was too embarrassed to move. Then
he felt someone shaking him.
"Wake up, Arthur!" said Buster. "The movie's over."

At lunch, Arthur didn't feel like eating.
"What should I do, Buster? Every time I go to sleep, I'm in my underwear!"
"Try staying awake," Buster suggested. "You can't dream if you don't sleep."

That night, Arthur tried some tricks to stay awake.

Old MacDonald had a farm...

But as hard as he tried,
Arthur just couldn't.

"I'll get you, Verminator....After...I take...a
little nap."

In Arthur's dream, the Verminator was torturing the class by scratching his claws on the blackboard. Hearing cries for help, Bionic Arthur rushed to the rescue!

But as he entered the classroom to take on the Verminator, everyone started laughing.

"My pants!" Arthur gasped as he woke up with a start. "Rise and shine, Mr. Fancy Pants," said D.W. "They're right here. Mom says you better shake a leg or you'll be late for school!"

Arthur asked Buster for some emergency advice on the way to school.

"It even happens when I'm a superhero!" he exclaimed. "I can't stay awake forever. I'm doomed!"

"Maybe you should sleep in your pants," said Buster. "That way you won't have to worry about putting them on."

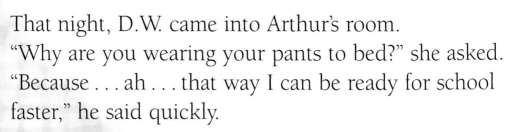

That night, D.W. came into Arthur's room.
"Why are you wearing your pants to bed?" she asked.
"Because . . . ah . . . that way I can be ready for school faster," he said quickly.

"I'm going to ask Mom if I can sleep in my clothes, too,"
D.W. said. "And maybe my coat and boots. *Mom?!*"
Arthur sighed and changed into his pajama pants.

The next day, Arthur was more worried than ever. "What if people find out about my underwear problem?" he asked Buster. "They'll call me names, and then I'll have to change schools. . . ."

"Don't worry," said Buster. "Your secret is safe with me."

At lunch the following day, Arthur sat with Francine and Muffy. They looked at him and started to giggle. "What's so funny?" Arthur asked.
"Do you have your pants on?" asked Francine. "Better make sure!"

Arthur checked. He *was* wearing pants.
He moved to another table.
"I heard about your nightmares," said the Brain, "so I got out a couple of books on dreams. Apparently, you have a pathological fear of embarrassment. . . ."

Arthur got up to find Buster.

"Buster!" cried Arthur. "You told everyone about my underwear dreams!"

"Not everyone," replied Buster. "Only a few kids."

"Buster, how could you?"

"Well, I couldn't help you. I needed some advice."

"This is so embarrassing!" said Arthur.

When Arthur turned to run out of the cafeteria,
his pants pocket got caught.

RRRIPPP!

Everyone in the cafeteria began to laugh.
Arthur couldn't move.
But Binky grabbed two trays to cover him.
"Quick!" he whispered. "Into the kitchen!"

Mrs. MacGrady wrapped her apron around Arthur and got out a needle and thread.

"I'm sorry," Buster said. "I shouldn't have told anyone."

"It's okay," said Arthur sadly. "You were just trying to help. The hard part will be telling my parents that I have to change schools."

Mrs. MacGrady handed Arthur his pants.

"Thanks," said Arthur. "Is there a back door?"

"Afraid not," said Mrs. MacGrady. "But do you know the old saying, 'A banana without its peel is still a banana'?"

"Huh?" said Arthur and Buster.

"It means people get embarrassed all the time," Binky explained.

"But you're still Arthur," said Mrs. MacGrady. "A smart, kind young man — with or without your pants."

Arthur smiled.

A few days later, Arthur met Buster at the Sugar Bowl.
"Well, no more underwear nightmares!" Arthur said.
"That's great!" said Buster. "I never thought that ripping
your pants in the cafeteria would be the thing to cure
you."
As they stood up to leave, Arthur looked at Buster and
frowned.
"Uh, Buster . . . I think you forgot something."

Buster woke up with a scream.
"Uh-oh," he sighed. "Here we go again!"